Even If I Spill My Milk?

ANNA GROSSNICKLE HINES

Even If I Spill My Milk?

CLARION BOOKS / New York

Clarion Books
a Houghton Mifflin Company imprint
215 Park Avenue South, New York, NY 10003
Text and illustrations copyright © 1994 by Anna Grossnickle Hines

Illustrations executed in colored pencil over marker on Arches hot press watercolor paper
Text is set in 14/17 pt. Palatino

Printed in the U.S.A.

Library of Congress Cataloging-in-Publication Data

Hines, Anna Grossnickle.
   Even if I spill my milk? / by Anna Grossnickle Hines.
      p. cm.
   Summary: Because Jamie doesn't want his parents to go to a party and leave
him with a babysitter, he tries to delay their departure with a series of questions.
   ISBN 0-395-65010-0
   [1. Separation anxiety—Fiction. 2. Mothers and sons—Fiction.]
   I. Title.
   PZ7.H572Ev 1994
   [E]——dc20   93-17438
                                                          CIP
                                                          AC

        WOZ 10 9 8 7 6 5 4 3 2 1

For Terri . . . forever.

"Mama! Mama! I don't want you and Papa to go to a party tonight. I want you to stay with me."

"It'll be all right, Jamie," Mama said. "Jenny will be with you, and Papa and I will see you in the morning for our special first-thing hugs."

"Would you stay and tuck me in, Mama? Please?"
"If you can be in bed in five minutes, I'll be happy to
tuck you in."

"Mama, will you love me forever?"
"Forever," Mama said.
"Forever and ever?"
"Forever and ever. Now if you want your milk, we'd better get downstairs."

"Will you love me even if I spill my milk?"

"Yes, Jamie."

"Even if I spill my milk on your special going-to-a-party dress?"

"Accidentally?"

"Uh-huh. Is it one minute yet, Mama?"

"Yes, just one minute. I'd be upset about the dress, but accidents happen sometimes."

"What if it wasn't an accident, Mama? What if I did it on purpose?"

"Then I'd know you were angry with me, and I'd be
angry too. We'd have to talk about it."
"And would you still go to the party?"

"Yes, I'd still go."
"But you'd still love me?"
"I'd still love you."
"How many minutes is it now, Mama?"
"It's two."

"If I said I didn't like you anymore and I ran away,
would you still love me?"
"Of course I would."
"What if I ran away and never came back?"

"Then I'd miss you and I'd try to find you."
"But you couldn't tuck me in, could you?"
"No."
"Is it three minutes yet?"
"Yes, it's three."
"What if you told me to go to bed and I didn't?"
"Then I'd have to pick you up and put you there."
"Would you still love me?"

"I'd still love you."

"What if I didn't kiss you good night?"

"I'd hope for a kiss tomorrow. It's four minutes, Jamie."

"Then I'll give you a kiss."

"Good, I like your kisses. It's four and a half now."

"Mama, I don't want you to go to the party, but I still love you."

"I know, and I love you, too. That's five, Jamie. You just made it."

"Mama, what if I don't go to sleep when you turn out the light?"

"Then I'll still say good night and go to the party."

"But will you come in and kiss me one more time when you get home?"

"Of course, but you don't have to stay awake for that.
I'll give you one more kiss even if you're sleeping."
"And Papa, too?"
"Papa, too."
"Okay, I'll go to sleep, but Mama?"
"What, Jamie?"

"Could Jenny read me a story? Please?"
"All right," said Mama, "but just one."

"Good night, Jamie."

"Good night, Papa. Good night, Mama.

"Okay, Jenny. Let's choose a long story and read it slow."